For Marguerita Rudolph (1908–1992)
Teacher, writer, friend of life—AHS

For my sister Marilyn—GC

Printed on recycled paper

A PaperStar Book, published in 1997 by The Putnam & Grosset Group,
200 Madison Avenue, New York, NY 10016. PaperStar Books
is a registered trademark of The Putnam Berkley Group, Inc.
The PaperStar logo is a trademark of The Putnam Berkley Group, Inc.
Originally published in 1994 by Philomel Books.
Published simultaneously in Canada.
Printed in the United States of America.
Library of Congress Cataloging-in-Publication Data
Scott, Ann Herbert. Hi / by Ann Herbert Scott:
illustrated by Glo Coalson. p. cm.
Summary: While waiting in line with her mother
at the post office, Margarita greets the patrons who
come in carrying different types of mail.
[1. Postal service — Fiction.] I. Coalson, Glo, ill.
II. Title. PZ7.S415Hi 1994[E]—dc20 91-42978 CIP AC
ISBN 0-698-11446-9
10 9 8 7 6 5 4 3 2 1

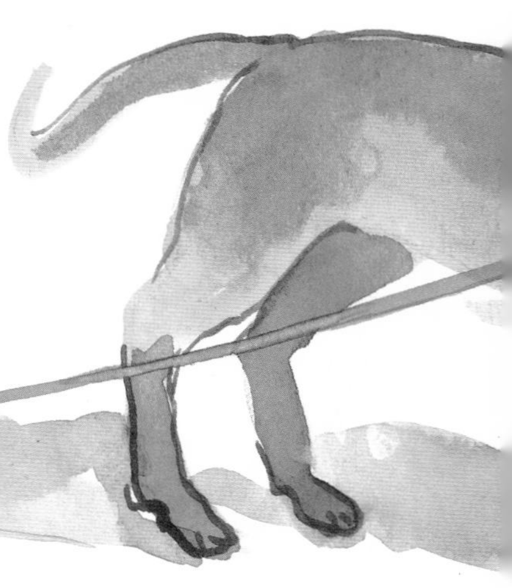

Hi

Ann Herbert Scott

Illustrated by

Glo Coalson

PaperStar

The Putnam & Grosset Group

Margarita and her mother wrapped a present for Margarita's grandmother and took it to the post office to mail.

They opened the big post office door and found a long line of people.

"Hi!" waved Margarita.

But nobody waved back. Nobody even noticed Margarita was there.

After a while the post office door swung open. In came an old man reading a newspaper.

"Hi!" called Margarita.

But the old man didn't notice Margarita. He was too busy reading his newspaper.

The door swung open again. Three girls hurried in to mail some postcards.

“Hi!” said Margarita.

But the girls didn't hear Margarita. They were too busy talking with each other.

After a while the door swung open again. In came a mother carrying a crying baby.

"Hi!" said Margarita.

But the mother didn't see Margarita. She was too busy taking care of her baby.

The door swung open for a boy with a tall pile of packages.

"Hi!" said Margarita, but not quite as loud as before.

But all the boy could see were his packages.

BABY

At last Margarita and her mother came to the front of the line.

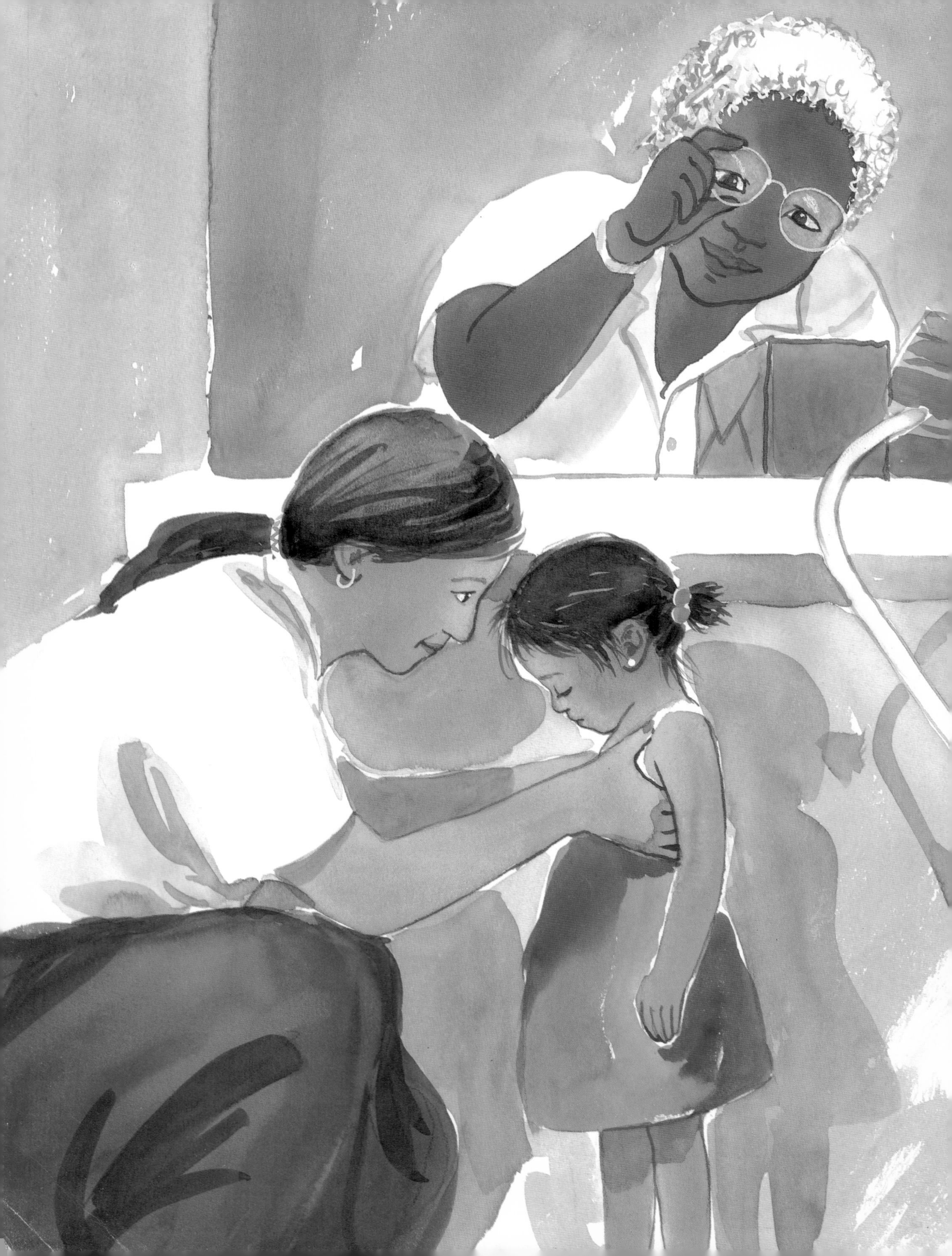

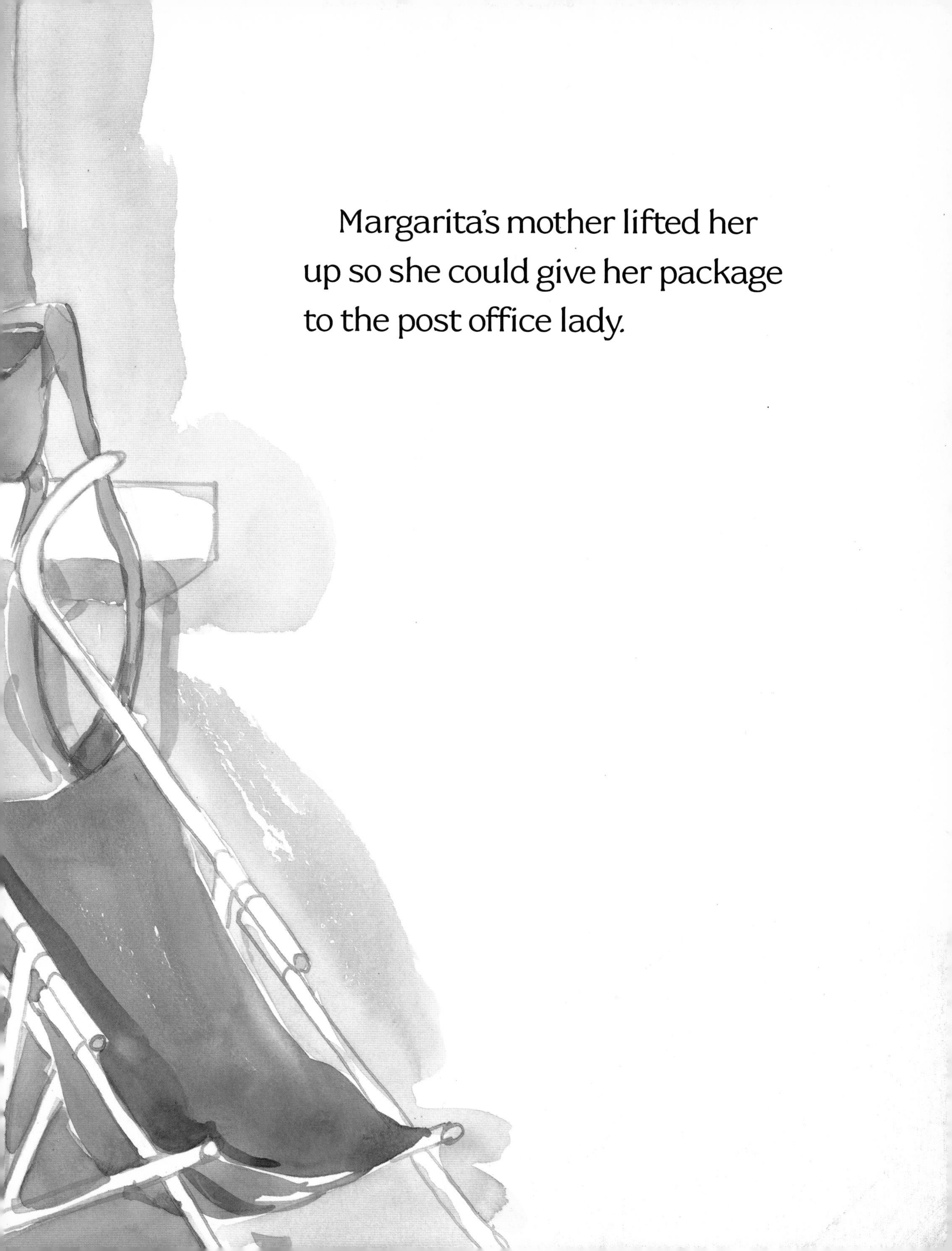

Margarita's mother lifted her up so she could give her package to the post office lady.

"Hi," whispered Margarita.

"Hi!" answered the lady, smiling right at her.

Margarita and her mother turned to go home.

"Bye!" said the post office lady with a big wave.

"Bye!" answered Margarita, waving back. And "Bye! Bye! Bye!" she called all the way to the post office door.